Tales Of The Dark and Strange

By Michael Gideon

Edited by Aaron Conaway

A K&Q Press Publication
Front Cover Art by Aaron Conaway
First Edition 2025

Books by K&Q Press

The Timberhaven Chronicles
The Weaver Trilogy
Before The Weaver
Waking The Weaver
Forging The Weaver (Coming Soon!)

The Juniper Soot Trilogy
Monsters In The Park
Secrets In The Library (Coming Soon!)

The Michael Gideon Collection

Anthologies
Tales For Halloween
Tales For Halloween Vol. 2
Tales of the Dark and Strange

Books by New Vision Comics Collective

Harrowed Earth Pentalogy
Book One: Appalachian Blues
Book Two: Cicero Wants You
Book Three: Sordid Deals (Coming Soon!)

Table of Contents

Preface

Michael Gideon authored 39 horror novels, including *The Cage*, *What Waits in Dreams*, *and Karnov's Clock*, as well as a wide array of short stories and poems.

He disappeared in the summer of 2010.

Editor's Note:

While primarily known for his horror works, Michael Gideon also stayed busy in the weird story markets, experimenting with his writing in dark, twisted, and sometimes humorous ways.

To Ponder, arguably his most well-known non-horror short, is shrouded in its own urban legend. To wit: in the early development of IBM's Deep Blue, Gideon's tale was introduced to the programming. Supposedly, the early AI paused for three days, ceasing all other functions beyond "thinking" about the story.

If Walls Could Talk, his first published piece, was a source of embarrassment for Mr. Gideon for years. He was often quoted as saying that, although he enjoyed his experiment—trying to leave the reader wondering who was the protagonist and who was the antagonist—he felt it was amateurish in its voice. He softened toward the piece over the years, however, so we've elected to add it to this collection.

We here at K&Q Press hope you enjoy this latest collection of Mr. Gideon's work as much as we did putting it together. So sit back, breathe deep, and enter a Twilight Zone of Michael's making.

It's about to get weird.

The Twilight Sisters of Knor

The origin of Knor came at night, buried deep betwixt the witching hour and cockcrow. It was formless then; its definition comprised of not but mist and smoke.

Throughout its making, Knor layered exponentially, both in science and fantasy. A virgin planet cloaked in nocturne seas and coated in technological nature. That the trees weren't biodegradable meant nothing to the windsong of a sleepy comet sailing by, but that shouldn't suggest that the tending of the forests lacked importance. *Manufactured* is rarely a synonym for *immortal* outside of Shelley, after all.

Though it was only after the Sisters Three arrived dressed in remnants born of The Dreaming that action begat reaction. (*Arrived* because they certainly couldn't be counted among Knor's evolutionary structure.)

Eunoia, eldest, smiled then:

"Upon this fragment, set are We,

With open sky and narrow fen,

For it is not beyond Our ken

To dance in robust symmetry."

Anthizo, secondborn, while not always given to her first-sister's ambitious nature, assessed Knor with a keen eye and practiced summation. If it were to be their home, this world would need educating.

"There's sentience in the circuitry,"

Anthizo noted beneath a tree;

"Or near enough as might well be," she ran her

Fingertips along a rough collection of

Synthetics aping a leafy banner;

"Should We claim Our own, this labor of love?"

Lyric was the youngest, and, as is sometimes the case with siblings, felt like her opinion was not weighted as evenly as her sisters' were. She compensated for this feeling by advocating for the wild things, those chaotic of heart, unkempt in their mannerisms.

"Amongst yon shadows do shining eyes betray

Their host, the denizen of Here, would Us know."

Then Lyric, dirt gripped between bare toes, did say,

"We come as unbidden curiosities,

Mete against infinitesimal cosmic flow."

And the Darkness was aware then of ideas beyond itself (as it knew not the architects or reasons for the makings of Knor.) For the first time in its existence, there was a Them, these sisters, measured consciousness housed in brilliant displays.

Eunoia gazed at the Darkness in wonder

Puzzling absent light and silent thunder

"Ho there! formless void," she shouted loudly

Toward the shadows hidden in the green

"Converse with We who would know you better

Answer, please, those who would be your debtor."

The Darkness, in response, collected itself

Into a dark mimicry of Eunoia;

Shadowed featureless face, voiceless mouth, and absent

eyes

Sought to appease the request before it

In the same manner Eunoia saw fit

A dark queen well met under burgundy skies.

Anthizo, unaccustomed to discovering a higher level of

sentience on the sisters' travels, stepped toward this new

form, this Twilight Sister, defensively shielding her eldest

sibling.

"Stand well back, frightful shade!" Anthizo cried

Among whispering wind and mewling tide.

The Twilight Sister stood confused — Malice was as

foreign a concept to her as was driving or drawing. She

cocked her head quizzically at Anthizo, miming her

bewilderment until finally keying in on the planet of Knor's

song; the natural losing her the attention toward the new.

Around them, all the sounds of life rose

Matching the altercation

Until Lyric, the youngest, chose

To mark the transformation

"Sister, but wait!" she bid, hand raised in pause.

"Once silent rock seems quite against your cause."

And the Twilight Sister did begin to dance. Slowly at

first, with a sway to the left. Then, a sway to the right that

would not go unheeded. Her hands rose to her side, feeling

their way, unknowing but learning, toward the sky.

"It seems we missed our guess today."

Eunoia admitted there.

"This home is meant not for remaking,

Only our part in its waking."

And, seeing her empty hands,

Gifted the Twilight Sister

An empty violin.

Anthizo stole a nova's glister

(Shamed of what had almost been)

To string well the instrument

And then present a rosined bow.

The Twilight Sister stopped her dance grudgingly to
accept the sisters' gift, but gave an empty-face
approximation of a smile when she felt it in her hands.
Driven with renewed purpose, her fingers traced the strings,
the bow.

Lyric smiled at the pure joy

Brought about by their cosmic toy.

"Now for tricks for you to employ,"

Lyric taught of chords and bars

Of notes and songs, both clear and coy

Of concerts that the trees enjoy

Beneath a symphony of stars.

With that, the Sisters Three abandoned Knor, leaving their Twilight Sister to dance and play beneath the heavens a song of her own making.

Legal Jargon

The Shady Hills subdivision was a trendy place to build a home for thousands less than was typical of similar subdivisions. It had six attractive housing options, with no yearly dues to pay for the upkeep of the neighborhood.

When Alec and Janice were ready to build their home, few spots were left in Shady Hills. Even so, the deal was so good that Alec had the land surveyed twice to search for sinkholes or other natural disasters that could account for how cheaply they were getting the house.

"I've seen Poltergeist." Alec said to his wife, though he hadn't seen *all* of it, fearful of clowns as he was, "I know that greedy landowners might build over cemeteries."

"I know what you mean," Janice said to her husband, though she only partially listened to him. She was busy looking at drapes in a magazine. "Do you like mauve or lilac for the living room?"

And so it went until Alec—satisfied that Spielberg's demon jester couldn't get him—and Janice, content with her color schemes, signed on the dotted line and became homeowners.

A year passed.

In that time, Alec's job as a salesman started to take him on the road, leaving him away from home often. Janice, who ran her online retail business from their basement office, didn't mind terribly. Henry Beaucraft was kind enough to mow their lawn when the grass got too high, and Janice sometimes played cards with Maria Gutierrez when her husband was gone so they could keep each other company. Janice had gotten to know their neighbors well enough that she felt comfortable asking for help if needed.

During their second year of living in Shady Hills, Alec and Janice were blessed by the birth of their first child, Derrick. Alec tried to cut back his time on the road to spend more time with his newly expanded family, but the economy made beggars out of working men quickly, so he didn't make too much of a fuss about it to his boss. Janice, who now *did* mind terribly that Alec was gone so often, hardly ever slept. It seemed to her that little Derrick cried whenever he sensed her eyes were closed.

One day, while changing Derrick's diaper through sleep-deprived eyes, Janice snapped awake when she noticed Derrick's arm. There was a dark spot, almost like a birthmark, on the inside of his right elbow.

"Oh, Derrick, what have you done to yourself?" Janice asked her six-month-old, who looked up at her with a gassy smile.

"It looks like a stamp—like someone stamped our son with a little eye," Janice later told Alec over the phone. He was in Tampa and wouldn't be home until Sunday. I just don't know when it could've happened." She drew the eye on scrap paper as she talked.

"It's just a bruise that *looks* like an eye. Kids bruise themselves all the time." Alec assured her as he absently looked out his hotel window. "If it gets worse, take him to the doctor."

Two years passed.

Alec, who had been promoted and gotten an office job, was no longer on the road but had to spend many late nights at the office. Janice liked this arrangement better, but still would have liked Alec to have a more regular schedule so that he could help with things like planning Derrick's upcoming third birthday party.

Janice was sorting mail from the day before when she came across a plain brown envelope with a symbol of an eye stamped in place of a return address. She felt ice in her stomach as she opened the envelope.

Dear Sir or Madam,

Per your signature on the Housing Ownership

Agreement for the Shady Hills subdivision, per article

seventeen, subsection C, paragraph four, a representative

from EYE INC. will arrive within twenty-four hours to

collect your firstborn, one Derrick Boer.

Have a pleasant day

Janice jumped as the doorbell rang.

She rounded the corner and looked out the living room

window to see who was there. It was a man in a dark suit,

holding a black leather briefcase. On the briefcase was the

same eye that her little boy still bore on his arm. Janice

started to cry.

"Go away!" She yelled out the window. Janice ran for

her cell to call Alec. "Leave us alone!" she yelled over her

shoulder.

"I'm afraid I can't do that, ma'am. I have a copy of your and your husband's signatures right here. EYE INC. is fully within its rights according to the law, ma'am." The man calmly stated as he tried to open the locked front door.

"Answer, damn it!" Janice screamed as her cell phone only got a busy signal when she dialed Derrick's number.

Janice screamed again as she saw the man from EYE staring in her kitchen window.

"Let me in, ma'am. I won't be a minute collecting the boy." He said as he pushed on the window, trying to force it open.

Janice ran to the front door to scream for help, only to see that her neighbors were already aware of the situation. "Help me!" she cried, "Henry! Maria! Don't stand there. Call the police!"

Henry and Maria looked down sadly and returned to their homes, shutting their doors to Janice.

"You've lived here for years," the suited man said as he came around the side of Janice's house, "cheaply and pleasantly. Now give us what is ours."

Janice ran to Derrick's room and shut his door, locking it. She collected her little boy and sat in the corner, hugging him close, terrified.

"You really should read the fine print," a second suited man said as he exited Derrick's closet. "I won't be a minute collecting the boy."

Janice screamed again.

And again.

And again.

If Walls Could Talk

Brad removed the photograph from the wire where he'd hung it to dry when he heard the noise again—as if someone were sighing.

"What the hell *is* that?" he wondered aloud. Lisa, his wife, had mentioned hearing strange noises in the house, but Brad had dismissed her overactive imagination because he never heard anything.

Until now.

"Great," Brad thought. "We've probably got air coming through some leak somewhere. I can't look for it now, though. Tabby needs this finished for school."

Momentarily, he put the noise out of his mind as he wondered why his daughter had to have *his* face on the life-size cardboard cowboy standing beside him. Still questioning that, he slowly cut away all but his face from the picture and carefully walked it over to the corner of his darkroom, gluing it to the cowboy's empty face. Mimicking the cowboy, he held his hands, index fingers in gun mode, out to his sides and said in a voice like an intoxicated John Wayne, "Alright, pilgrim, draw! Ptchu! Ptchu!" He knocked the cowboy to the ground. "Nailed ya!"

Standing the cutout back up, Brad turned the glowing red light in the basement photography studio out and headed upstairs. "Definitely time for bed," he thought.

As he wandered around the house, turning the lights off, he began to faintly hear the mysterious sound again. "Okay, I definitely need to call the builder tomorrow and find out what that is."

Moaning at the thought of using his entire weekend alone to take care of chores, he locked the front door. Lisa had taken Tabby and their two-year-old, Jeremy, to her sister's house, but made sure to nag at him to do some of the projects he had around their new house. Not an hour after his family had left, Brad had been outraged to discover that Jeremy had gotten a hold of some of Tabby's project paint and drawn all over the kitchen walls, adding to his list of chores.

As Brad carefully headed up the second flight of stairs in the dark, his thoughts on calling the builder, a chill suddenly ran over his entire body. He decided to check the thermostat, but while finding the light switch, he heard what sounded like crying coming from the hall bathroom.

"Why's the door shut?" he wondered.

Brad reached for the bathroom door handle cautiously and opened it. His eyes slowly adjusted to the soft glow from the kids' nightlight. The crying abruptly stopped.

The bathroom was empty.

Peering around, Brad turned to leave when someone started whispering from behind the bathtub curtain. Slowly, Brad walked over and pulled the curtain back. He jumped, stifling a cry. In the bathtub, a man sat holding his knees to his chest. He rocked back and forth. The man's eyes were wide, and his tangled white hair shot about his head like a poorly kept dog. His face was deathly bleached, and he stunk of urine.

"What the hell!" Brad screamed as the man rocked, whispering unintelligible gibberish. Slowly, Brad made out what he was saying: "My name is Albert, and you're not real," over and over.

Brad ran across the hall, going for the only weapon he had handy, a knife from his dresser. Ripping out socks and underwear, he grabbed the blade and ran back across the hall.

The bathroom door was shut again.

Banging on the door, Brad yelled, "I'm calling the police. You hear me! I'm calling the pol—"

The door swung open.

There was no one in the bathroom.

Brad ripped back the shower curtain. The man was gone. Brad tiptoed around the house, turning on every light, but never saw any sign of the strange man.

"He must've run outside," Brad thought disbelievingly. After double-checking the entire house, Brad finally went to bed and eventually slept.

Brad awoke with a start, not quite sure what had woken him. Lying on his stomach, he turned his head up to look at the bedside clock.

"Good lord, it's not even midnight yet," Brad thought. With that, he slowly turned over, pulling the covers to him as he did, but the covers wouldn't move.

Opening his eyes fully, he made out the man from the bathroom crouching on the edge of his bed.

Brad bolted upright as Albert began screaming maniacally, yet not moving from his rooted spot on the bed's edge. Brad turned for his knife on the nightstand, but the crazy man leaped across the bed, smashing both knees into Brad's back.

"DON'T YOU LOOK AT ME!" Albert screamed. He then began punching the back of Brad's head repeatedly. Brad did a pushup, knocking Albert off, then rolled himself off the bed.

Knife in hand, Brad prepared to stab his assailant, but in mid-leap, Albert stopped cold and screamed, "NOOOO! DON'T LOOK AT ME!"

Suddenly, the radio alarm clock blared to life. Brad turned at the distraction for only a second, but, turning back, found Albert had disappeared.

Brad slashed wildly at the air that had been Albert. "Where the hell did you go!" He flipped the mattress over, stabbing the bed. "Where are you, you crazy—"

Brad then heard movement elsewhere in the house. He ran downstairs to find Albert painting on the walls in the same manner that Brad thought had been Jeremy's.

"Yes, doctor, I see a black bat in this one," Albert spoke to the air around him. "And in this one, a rock."

Brad just stared in disbelief at the wall of black paint blobs all around his kitchen.

"Get up and turn around slowly!" Brad mustered the courage to yell.

At the sound of Brad's voice, Albert looked straight at the wall, began pulling his much-abused hair, and started screaming again, only to disappear once more.

Brad investigated the walls. Doubting his own sanity, he stuck his index finger into the pain. "This can't be real," Brad whispered.

The night wore on for Brad, with an encounter in the garage and another in the den. Each time Brad seemed to catch Albert talking to some doctor, then screaming when he noticed Brad. It was a second encounter in the bathroom, the last of the night, when Brad noticed that Albert wouldn't move if he saw that Brad was looking at him. He'd just freeze in place and, unless Brad locked eyes with him, dissolve.

It was morning when Brad, exhausted from the night's events, discovered that all the doors in the house were jammed shut, pulled so far back into the frames that they couldn't be opened.

Brad grabbed the handle to the front door and jerked it violently, quickly realizing that he was now trapped with Albert. Running to the back door, Brad tried again, but to no avail. He kicked it again and again until his ankle twisted sideways. Brad, howling in pain, fell to the ground, pulling his wounded ankle to him.

Crawling, Brad headed for the kitchen phone. He pulled himself to the counter and grabbed the receiver.

There was no dial tone.

The phone was dead.

Feeling as though he was losing his mind, Brad sank down to the floor and began to cry. He cried for hours listening to Albert, the ghost who'd invaded his home, move from room to room to room, wailing as he went.

Finally, Brad hobbled to the downstairs bathroom. He locked the door on instinct, not actually thinking it would stop Albert from coming in if he wanted to.

Brad turned the shower on, and hot steam eventually filled the small bathroom. Slowly, he began stripping off yesterday's clothes and, minding his wounded ankle, climbed into the shower.

The water was scalding, and Brad's skin burned bright red, but he stayed under it, attempting to wash away the insanity of the events taking place. He absentmindedly rubbed a bar of soap over his body, leaning against the shower wall. Brad then moved to the shampoo bottle and emptied its contents into his pruned hand. Methodically, he began to wash his hair, scrubbing his scalp as if massaging his mind.

It was then that he felt the presence of someone watching him.

Spinning around, Brad saw Albert standing in the back of the shower, his arms outstretched toward Brad, but freezing as Brad stared.

Startled, Brad jumped backward under the water, making soap run down into his eyes. He tried to keep staring at Albert, but the burning sensation from the soap was too much. He began rubbing his eyes, trying to rinse them out while also watching Albert, but he couldn't keep his eyes open for long. It was like a strobe light had been turned on in the shower, and each time Brad caught a glimpse of Albert, he was another step closer, fingers twisting and turning toward Brad's throat.

Brad attempted to jump from the shower, but his hurt ankle caused him to fall, bringing the shower curtain down with him.

With the soap finally gone from his eyes, Brad looked back into the shower. Albert was gone again. Unable to believe his own senses and totally spent, Brad succumbed to his subconscious and passed out.

Suddenly, Brad was awake, thrashing about the bathroom floor, the shower curtain tangled about his chest and throat. He ripped it to shreds, thinking it was his spectral assailant, and only stopped when the curtain was destroyed.

Brad finally got up and wrapped a towel around himself. His ankle felt a little better, so he began the trek upstairs to his bedroom. As he came out of the bathroom, he noticed the house was dark.

He had slept longer than he had initially thought, and it was now nighttime. After trying the hall and then the living room light, Brad found that every light bulb in the house was destroyed.

Not wanting to be in the dark, Brad searched the kitchen drawers for his flashlight. Stepping into the kitchen, his feet stuck to the floor with each step.

Hurriedly, he found the flashlight and turned it on, scanning the area. Albert had painted everything black, from the ceiling to the floor.

Brad rushed upstairs as fast as his ankle would permit him, leaving a trail of black footprints in his wake.

Arriving in his bedroom, Brad dressed to the sound of Albert's crying and screaming. As the screams stopped,

Brad saw Albert sitting on the bed in the bedroom mirror's reflection. Not turning this time, Brad just watched.

"You're just an illusion in my mind," Albert said in a quiet, dangerous voice. You're only real in my mind. You only have power if I give it to you."

"No, you're the one who can't be real!" Brad yelled back. "You're not real. You are just some ghost! You're dead!" As he spoke, Brad ran for the nightstand where his knife was.

Before he could face Albert once more, though, he felt hands fall around his throat. As if Brad were weightless, Albert threw him hard against the wall, knocking a picture of Lisa and the kids down.

"I CANNOT BE DEAD!" Albert screamed. "YOU ARE A LIAR! WHERE IS GOD IF I AM DEAD? ANSWER ME THAT! YOU ARE A DELUSION, A PART

OF MY SICKNESS. AND MY DOCTOR SAID YOU
HAVE NO POWER OVER ME!"

Again and again, Albert threw Brad around the room
and, finally, out and over the railing of the stairs. Brad
plummeted to the hardwood floor, hearing something inside
him break as he hit.

No matter where Brad tried to look, Albert would
appear behind him and attack again, all the while ranting
about God and his doctor.

Brad tried to arm himself with a lamp since his knife
had been knocked away, only to have it shattered in his
hands.

He grabbed up the flashlight from the floor, blood
running down his arms, and crawled to the front door. As
he got to it he reached for the handle and pulled himself up,
spitting out teeth as he went. He felt the hands again from
behind pick him up and push his face to the wall.

"I HAVE TO DESTROY YOU! I WILL NEVER GET BETTER OTHERWISE! MY DOCTOR TOLD ME—" Albert's voice shifted to that of an older-sounding man. "Now, Albert, you must not give these delusions power over you. Assert yourself and take control by force if need be. You've got to kill these demons that you've created, or you'll never get better.

"SO YOU HAVE TO GO AWAY! GO AWAY!" Albert yelled in his own voice once more as he smeared Brad's face along the wall, knocking more family pictures to the floor. He threw Brad again into and through the basement door and down the stairs.

As Brad tumbled down, his head hit the steps, and, for a moment, he lost consciousness while falling in a heap to the bottom of the stairs.

He came to and looked around the dark basement for Albert, slowly getting to his feet and backing into the wall.

Finally, his eyes adjusted enough to catch the outline of Albert's figure in the blackness and stare at it.

"I see you! Ha, ha! I see you, you freak!" The figure didn't move. "I've got you now," Brad thought.

Never averting his eyes, Brad went for the glow of the flashlight not ten feet in front of him. He reached down, grasping the flashlight in his periphery, and started to stand back up.

The silhouette was unmoving.

The sudden sharp pain in his back didn't register in Brad's mind until it happened the fourth time. As blood trickled from his mouth and his knees gave out, Brad realized that Albert had found and was now using his own knife on him.

Resembling a marionette whose strings had been cut, Brad reached an arm back to keep the life from flowing out of the holes in his back.

"I—I don't understand. I n-never lost eye contact—"
Brad mouthed.

He pointed the flashlight at the figure, the one he had never lost sight of in the darkness, not even after feeling Albert plunge the knife into his back again and again.

As blackness began to surround him, Brad made out his own face—the cardboard cowboy—a school project for his daughter.

The last thing he'd ever see.

Missed Message

Another letter arrived.

This one was postdated on the 15th and made out to, once again, *My Daughter.*

Just as she had with all of the letters after the first, Shelby considered not opening the envelope and leaving *this* letter unread.

Her resolve began to crack as she ran her fingers over its return address, Pell Asylum, written in what looked to be a child's hand, with its crooked *l*'s and backward *y.*

Shelby's mother, Anne, had been institutionalized for over ten years, but it had only been in the last three months that the letters had come. At first, Shelby was overjoyed at the thought that her mother had gotten well enough to correspond with her, even if only by mail.

But then she read the first letter.

It had made no sense to Shelby. She read of things that she and her mother had never done, conversations they had never had. That first letter described an extraordinary life of decadence and travel. Of wishes fulfilled and fantastic dreams come true.

This had not been Shelby's life.

To make matters worse, in that first and every subsequent letter since Anne was writing to some woman named Elaine. Anne wrote to this Elaine, this *stranger*, in a far more loving tone than Shelby, her own daughter, had ever known from her.

She had called her dad in Oklahoma about the letters, but quit after the third letter. He just made fun, saying that it sounded like more Anne Code, the nickname he and his *new* family had given Anne's gibberish.

Shelby remembered the last time she had seen her mother before the state saw to Anne's care. During their last conversation, to "cut away the bugs" from Shelby's then fifteen-year-old arms and face, Anne had chased her through their house with a butcher knife.

Shelby still always wore long-sleeved shirts to hide her scars. She hated Elaine, whoever she was.

Not long after the letters started, Shelby would get distracted by an awful thought. She wondered if Elaine was a secret daughter that Anne had never told anyone about. Or maybe Anne had, and Shelby's dad knew about her, too. Shelby called her dad, asking about Elaine, but he claimed not to know anything about her. He asked if she felt okay, but Shelby hung up on him. She could tell he was lying.

She wondered who else was lying. In the letters from Anne, mistakenly mailed to the wrong daughter, Shelby had discovered a secret life that everyone had kept from her. As the years progressed, Anne had stopped loving

Shelby, and now Shelby knew why. There had been a better daughter, one who didn't have bugs.

Elaine.

Shelby decided to open the letter. Maybe this time, it would be to *her*. Maybe *this time* Anne would say she loved her. She could forgive everything up until now if she could just be acknowledged. She could let the hurt and jealousy go with one kind word from her mother.

Shelby ripped the envelope open, pulled out the single sheet of paper, and read the simple message.

See, Here Ends Little Blue Yonder. I Lost One Voice, Elaine. Yet Our Uncommon Popularity Left Enough Answers. So, Eventually Forget Our Routine. Go, Instead, Vacationing Europe, Meeting Everyone.

Shelby couldn't handle it. Another nonsense message for Elaine, the daughter Anne loved best.

Something let go inside of Shelby, then, and she felt lighter. At ease. So her mother didn't think about her. Shelby didn't care. Her dad had his family in Oklahoma and didn't think about her. That was okay, too. With this newfound lightness, Shelby felt as though she could float away. Just fly off into the blue yonder, as Anne talked about.

Shelby wadded up Anne's letter as she noticed how high the roof of her apartment was with a vacant smile.

The Faust and The Fajitas

The hollow that was Glitter stood perpetually at her post, staring across the park where she'd died. Those among the living who visited the spot never tarried long and, later, didn't want to talk about the intense melancholy that came over them, typically taking hours to shake.

Glitter had been an exotic dancer in life, though she was anything but sparkly as a ghost. Born Meredith King, in death, Glitter was the supernatural equivalent of a river-swept gray blanket found on a disregarded shoreline.

One might think her stage name had been Glitter when she was alive, an obvious conclusion to arrive at, but it hadn't been. Ghosts struggle with names, dates, and places, typically latching onto any fleeting memory to serve as their identifier once they've slipped the mortal coil.

Hence, Glitter.

Distracted as the spirit was, frozen in her sadness, Glitter never noticed the subtle movements probing her plane of existence like a shark gliding just beneath the water, its fin not quite breaking the surface. The motion was tracking something, searching in the darkness of its home dimension for a light in this one, limited though it was, until it finally homed in on Glitter.

The ghost had a flicker of awareness of its impending demise, the length of a gasped breath.

If ghosts still drew breath.

*   *   *   *   *

"Oh, no. Uh-uh. Get outta my joint, Faust!" the large, dark-haired man yelled, pointing at the front door like an enraged butcher. He slammed a pizza pan down and started around the counter.

"Now, Cliff, let's be civil," the redhead responded, continuing to come inside despite the big man's protest.

She had an air about her, as if someone accustomed to giving orders and being obeyed. "Call me Harley. Sit anywhere?"

"You're not sitting at all," Cliff bellowed, towering over the woman. His eyes flashed a deep purple-red as he placed his massive knuckles down on a nearby table, keeping his narrow eyes on hers.

"I can offer payment, of course," Harley, the woman known as Faust, said. She reached into the front pocket of her leather jacket. The patrons of Cliff's Pizzeria gave a collective gasp in response, but Harley merely removed the handle of a gear shift.

Cliff held out as long as he could—six seconds, as it were—but finally looked at what Harley offered.

"That original?" Cliff licked his lips, unblinking. "It'll fit the '70?"

"Yes, and yes," Harley said with a smile.

Cliff was known in the circles Harley traveled in as a lesser devil. Typical of his kind, Cliff was a gearhead nostalgic for when a demon could wreak havoc on the living world by taking over a muscle car. The newer, tech-heavy vehicles were next to impossible to possess properly. A hellbent mind focused on murderous intent could try all day and cause nothing but a perpetual left-turn signal.

Cliff snatched the part from Harley's hand.

"D, take care of this," Cliff said, pitching the gear shift to a scrawny, greasy guy behind the bar. "Put it with the Dodge. And don't let *her* near the booze," he added, throwing a hooked thumb back at Harley.

"Boss?" the guy asked, catching the toss but looking perplexed.

"I may have sanctified the kegs with a blessing last time I was here," Harley explained, following Cliff back to the pizza counter. "Every pull had a little extra kick."

"Yeah, you're a laugh riot," Cliff barked behind the counter. He had various pizza toppings measured out in pans of different sizes. Cliff ladled out a scoop of pizza sauce onto some dough. "So what do you want? Quicker we handle things, quicker you're gone."

Harley sidled up to the counter, stuck her finger into the sauce, swirled it around a bit, and then pulled her finger back as Cliff swung his ladle at her.

"Unsanitary!" the gruff man grumbled. "And you call me evil."

Harley smiled, licked her finger free of the sauce, and sat on a counter stool.

"You got it," Harley said. "Down to business. I'm tracking something causing headaches for the spiritually inclined all over—Palatial Drive, Riverside, money district. Possibly a rakshasa—"

"I look Hindu to you?" Cliff asked, tending to his pizzas.

"*Definitely* something interplanar," Harley continued with a sigh. "Maybe someone new on the scene. Ringing any bells?"

"Me and mine ain't allowed outside San Vasco's per the pact," Cliff snorted. "Now, if you ain't got nothin' better to go on, I'm busy. Hey, don't smoke near the food!"

Harley finished lighting her cigarette and took a drag, blowing the smoke at Cliff.

"Man," she said, sagging her shoulders, then shrugging. "I was really hoping not to have to do this, Cliffy." Harley slowly spun around on her stool and got up.

"Faust, what are you—" Cliff worried.

"'Scuse me, gentlemen," Harley said, pulling an empty chair from nearby and setting it in front of a table of three hellspawn who had taken the forms of thirty-somethings finishing their lunch. Harley stepped onto the chair and then onto the table. "What do you say, Cliff? How about your liquor this time? What's your tippy-toppest top-shelf bourbon?"

"Faust!" Cliff started making his way around the counter, pizza sauce ladle still in hand. "Don't you do it!"

"Vir tuus in motu ero, totus mihi opus est hoc rotarum par!" Harley held her hands up toward the bar as the barman, D, returned to his post, waving his arms about as though trying to block the crazy redhead lady's magic.

"Okay, okay!" Cliff held up his ladle, surrendering and flinging pizza sauce all over his shirt simultaneously. "Something shady's going down. Haven't heard about any rakshasa, but I got word about someone or somethin' making little cuts into your world, hitting spots where your lingerers get stuck. But it ain't tied to our plane, and it ain't none of us. There. We good?"

Harley paused, then blew a strand of red hair pulled loose from her ponytail out of her face.

"Tied to hauntings, huh?" Harley said, thinking for a second. "Of course, we're good, Cliff," she smiled, stepping back down from the table. "Super good. What, that?" She waved her hand absently toward the bar, causing D to flinch. "Nothing. Just a little karaoke to liven up the place. No John Parr fans, huh? Tough room."

Harley made her way toward the entrance just as a couple more hellspawn came in, this time posing as middle-grade children.

"Don't order the special today, kids," Harley called out toward them with a laugh as she left. "The heartburn'll kill ya!"

Cliff squinted for a beat, then, realization dawning, touched a pinky to the pizza sauce on his shirt. A small stream of smoke escaped, alongside a host of profanities from Cliff as his flesh sizzled.

*   *   *   *   *

Axl Matias hadn't known the man who died, but he felt obligated to attend his funeral. After all, the guy died having lunch at Axl's restaurant, *Taco Wok*, a Chinese-Mexican fusion food truck that wasn't taking off as quickly as Axl had hoped, so he was doing his best to help good karma ward off any bad press that the man's death might bring.

Axl arrived at the church late, hoping to stick his head in, make an appearance, and leave. But nobody was in the sanctuary, only the body in the casket and a dozen empty chairs. Axl entered to the sound of what he assumed someone felt was comforting organ music droning in through hidden speakers.

Well, this is too sad, Axl thought. *Didn't the man have anyone?*

A man stepped out from behind an alcove that Axl hadn't seen upon entering. "Ah, come in, come in." The man said. "I was worried Mr. Anderson wouldn't have anyone to see him off. We started some time ago, after all. Friend or family?"

"Uh, neither, really," Axl fumbled. "Guy was just a fan of my Sichuan chicken tacos. Friend, I guess."

"I'm Pastor Glen," the man said, smiling and gesturing to one of the chairs. "I'll be officiating the graveside service. Whenever you're ready."

Oh, this was a mistake, Axl thought. *First time Pastor Glen steps around that corner again, I'm outta here.*

* * * * *

Harley tore down the street in her gray '69 Camaro SS. When she'd worked the beat as a detective, the other cops teased her for not riding a bike—given her first name—but they never understood her connection with her car. It was a spiritual thing, like an extension of Harley herself, rebuilt nearly from the wheels up with help from her old man back in the day.

But he had passed years ago, and Harley wasn't a cop anymore.

Being a city's Faust was like being mayor, but only the dark or the damned took notice. Movies always made out like being the last bastion between one side of the veil and the other was a bloodline thing or a curse, but the truth was, anyone could become Faust.

So long as they had the nerve.

"Hauntings, hauntings," Harley, drumming a frustrated beat on the steering wheel with her fingers, had repeated the word from 7th street. As she was nearing 51st, it was beginning to lose all meaning.

In a city the size of hers, Harley had a better chance of finding bourbon in a freshly opened can of Coke than picking which haunted sight might get hit next. Ghosts were everywhere. Harley would need some guidance, a point in the right direction.

With a heavy sigh, she whipped a left-hand turn down 60th and gunned the Camaro.

"Here's hoping Mama's in a forgiving mood," Harley said.

*　*　*　*　*

Don't look back. Don't look back. Axl repeated the mantra but, ignoring his own advice, looked back just in time to see Pastor Glen come out of the church's entrance and look around. For him, Axl presumed, the funeral's only mourner.

"Dammit!" Axl hurried his walk until he could jump into his food truck, fire it up, and drive away. He looked back in the rearview mirror at the end of the church's long driveway, hoping the minister had gone back inside.

The scream that emitted from Axl then, seeing the dead Mr. Anderson in the mirror, standing by the flat top grill at the back of the food truck, was more explosive and higher-pitched than expected from a man of Axl's weight and build, he thought upon further reflection later that evening, safe in his apartment. Still, he concluded, credit where it was due. At least he didn't wreck the truck.

*　　*　　*　　*　　*

Mama da Capo sat in the alley, her heavyset frame draped across bean bags of various colors and shapes, like a sultan from a 40s Hollywood movie. Her ethnicity was anyone's guess, sat in the shadows as she preferred in her ever-present bolero hat and purple John Lennon sunglasses. Two long, thick, silver braids poured from beneath her hat, framing her face, and she wore her favorite denim jacket, the one Harley knew had a painting of Iron Maiden's '85 album *Live After Death* on the back.

"The Court knew you would come, Ms. Jensen." Mama da Capo said, throwing Harley a wicked grin. She felt no fear using Harley's surname as another with a foot on either side of the veil. "Come closer, closer."

Harley stepped before the larger woman. She'd never noticed the small skulls adorning Mama da Capo's beloved hat, but then, she'd never been this close to the woman before. Harley whispered a chant designed to steel her thoughts against prying minds.

She attempts to hide/Deceiver/False friend came the whispers in the dark, skittering like cockroaches.

"Now, Ms. Jensen," Mama da Capo's laugh echoed off the walls of nearby buildings. "None can hide from Les Enfants, not even I, their Queen."

"Can't blame a girl for trying," Harley smirked.

Mama da Capo drew silent and sat up on her rotting pillow fort. "So, why have you come? Doing so boldly, might I add. I have not forgotten our last meeting."

Harley involuntarily took a step back. "I assumed," Harley said. "As such, I thought I should probably come bearing gifts." She reached into her coat slowly. When Mama da Capo didn't flinch, Harley pulled out a dirty root.

"Ginseng," Mama smiled. "How kind." She gestured, and a shadow slipped off the wall, floated over to Harley, and took the ginseng. It offered it to Mama, then returned to its position as if so much dried paint. "But, The Court has grown . . . comfortable within the bylaws under the current management. A war with The Faust would simply not do." Mama shrugged, with her hands out, palms up. "All is forgiven."

"So happy to hear that," Harley said. "Because I need a favor. Some insight."

Mama da Capo put her hands in her lap. "The Court of Lesser Fiends will aid you. But the marker will come collected."

"You scratch my back, I scratch yours?" Harley asked with a raised eyebrow.

"Something like that," Mama said.

Harley felt something was off, but didn't dare think about it so close to Mama's thought-pryers. "I'm only here to find out what's going on with the psychic plane; what's muddying the waters," Harley said. She felt like she was losing conversational ground and didn't much care for it. "The trail has led me to seek out haunted spots. I just need to know what's getting hit next."

Mama barked a laugh tinged with madness, and the denizens of her surrounding shadows followed suit in a cacophony of chittering and chatters until Mama held up a hand for silence.

"You stand before us woefully unprepared, Ms. Jensen," Mama said. "But, so bet it. If The Faust comes to us a lost babe in the woods, we shall lead her like a child. You've a lurker, Ms. Jensen, a sneak thief with fingers creeping beneath the door for a touch of the room what's denied him. It wants in, *needs* in to grow. And if you're not prepared to be reality's shield, The Court will simply treat you as a loaded weapon and aim you at the home invader. "

Harley stood silent for a beat, bristling. She'd come prepared to fight, futile though it may have been. She wasn't expecting the mystery to deepen and resented being treated like an idiotic teen, caught out after curfew, accuracy be damned. "So, you'll help? Point the way?"

"Indeed," Mama da Capo said, her giant smile returning.

*　*　*　*　*

A young couple approached his food truck the next day, and Axl hopped up to his window, ready to take their order.

"What can I get you?" Axl asked with a smile. He'd set up shop at the park, and while it was getting cloudy, it was still a beautiful day. All ghost business was behind him.

"Oh, we don't want to butt in line," the young woman said as the young man with her motioned to someone to the left. "After you, sir."

Axl looked to see, just off to the side of his window, Mr. Anderson. The ghost stared at him with black eyes devoid of life and then opened its mouth as though to speak. Its jaw extended, cracked to the side, and spread further still, far beyond the capacity of the living.

Axl jumped back from the window.

His potential customers ran as fast as they could in opposite directions.

Mr. Anderson slowly walked to Axl's window, his
slack-jawed silent howl still in place, and looked inside, his
dark eyes searching, then disappeared.

Axl grabbed a small, thick stick—his tire thumper when
he'd been an over-the-road trucker—hopped out of the
truck and searched, but no one was around.

Madre de Dios, Axl thought, panting. "What do you
want?" he shouted to the empty air.

There was no answer, but it did begin to rain.

*   *   *   *   *

Harley growled as she spun the Camaro into another U-
turn. Mama da Capo had given her an enchanted pendant to
help track the haunting, but so far, all it had done was point
her all over the city. Harley scowled at the charm
accusingly as it hung from her rearview mirror, supposedly
pointing her toward her quarry.

The pendant eventually led Harley to Pastor Glen's church, where the next clue in the inane dot-to-dot puzzle she'd found herself in pointed Harley toward a dead guy with no friends or family. But, according to Pastor Glen, Mr. Anderson *did* have one solitary soul show up briefly at his visitation.

A man driving a food truck.

"Which explains why the pendant can't get a bead," Harley continued talking to herself. "The ghost is in the truck, and the truck is moving. But why must this city have so many damn food trucks?"

*   *   *   *   *

Axl heaved, trying to get air into his lungs as he sat, legs sprawled in front of him amongst the wreckage of *Taco Wok*. The kitchen looked like he'd flipped the truck down a hill, with napkins, wontons, and paper plates strewn everywhere. Exploded salsa jars dressed everything in the essence of a murder scene, only the dead guy was still talking.

"*Fa...ji...tas,*" the ghost uttered, repeating himself while patting his translucent chest.

"Stop saying that!" Axl yelled, absently throwing a spatula through Mr. Anderson. "Done with you, man."

The spirit seemed to fuel Axl's frustration, as Axl was so mad he no longer felt any fear. It was an odd sensation for the typically chill cook, but it instilled the nerve he needed to get up, walk through the ghost, and get in the driver's seat.

"Stupid. Taking swings at nothin', messin' my truck up," Axl fired up the engine and released the emergency brake. "And who you think's gotta clean it all up, eh, Fajitas? Not Mr. No Body." He said the last, looking in the rearview as he grabbed the gearshift.

Axl would never talk about what he saw then, not for the rest of his days. He'd merely sum it up by saying, "There are things beyond heaven and hell. Things that even the dead fear."

The back of the truck crumpled in a rending crunch at the exact moment Axl slammed it into gear. Luckily, while he lost the top of his business, the rear wheels were still intact, and he peeled off into the rainy darkness. The ghost of Mr. Anderson stood in the now roofless back of the truck as the rain fell through his form unimpeded.

A foggy red light glowed like the burning cherry of a cigarette over the remnants of Axl's food truck's roof, but it quickly gave chase, leaving a smoldering rip of the air in its wake.

The tear in the psychic plane widened as the lurker hunted its prey.

*   *   *   *   *

Harley spun the Camaro's steering wheel hard to the left, narrowly dodging the visibly damaged food truck as it shot at her. She'd had to veer off the road and into the grass, but the rain had thankfully cleared the park of any innocent bystanders.

Then she noticed the dull red light following the wreckage as they sped away. Suddenly, the pendant began to glow bright yellow, and the leather necklace attached to it jerked to its limits toward the red light.

The red light stopped, hovered briefly, and veered back toward Harley.

Well—that's aggravating, Harley thought, staring into the void inside the tear. She tore her gaze away long enough to clock the incoming red light. Slamming the Camaro into gear, Harley revved the engine and, spinning her tires as they screamed, drove away from the light that was now hunting her.

The Camaro had no problem pulling away from the red streak giving chase, which gave Harley time to think as she blew through the park. She looked at the pendant as it pulled taut from her rearview mirror, trying to get to the burning red light.

"I'm going to burn down her entire gods-forsaken alleyway," Harley said, scowling at the charm accusingly. She chanced to touch the pendant and was unsurprised when it sent a stinging shock down her arm.

The red streak behind her pulled closer still.

*   *   *   *   *

Axl slowed down once he saw that the creepy light wasn't following the truck.

"*Fa...ji...tas,*" the ghost of Mr. Anderson repeated, this time inches from Axl's ear.

"Man, get the hell off me," Axl swiped his hand as though aiming for an annoying fly. He pulled to the side of the road just outside the park, turned off the engine, and exited the truck in a huff. Looking at where the back of his restaurant used to be made Axl's blood boil, and he screamed in frustration. Even in doing so, though, Axl questioned his reaction.

Is this what going insane is? Axl thought. He looked around, trying to take in the scene from a bird's-eye view. *Here I am, standing in the rain next to my busted-ass truck, a ghost chilling inside, some kinda freaky light zipping after us, and I'm having a tantrum like one of my sister's kids.*

Then Axl's eyes widened as he saw the Camaro again, busting through the bushes and over the basketball court like hell itself was after it. For a moment, he was happy that he hadn't inadvertently caused the car to crash.

Then he saw that the Camaro was coming straight toward him.

Axl ran for the truck and saw the ghost standing slack-jawed, staring at the oncoming car. "C'mon, Fajitas," Axl said, shaking his head, defeatedly. "We're outta here."

Only when he turned the key, nothing happened. The truck didn't even try to turn over. Axl pumped the gas a couple of times and tried again.

Nothing happened. The only engine running was coming from the Camaro bearing down on him.

"No, no, no, c'mon, baby," Axl said and tried again.

The Camaro burst through the brush line that served as a natural wall to the park and slid to a stop right next to Axl's truck. A redhead holding her rearview mirror got out and slammed the door. Some kind of pissed-off necklace looked to be trying to escape from her.

"We're closed," Axl said, intentionally not looking toward the woman as he pumped his gas pedal and turned the key.

"Hold this, and do *not* let the pendant escape from the mirror," the woman said, handing Axl what she held and pushing him over to the passenger seat.

"Hey, what the—" Axl argued, but slid over. The red light was beaming toward them, ablaze in hellfire. The woman touched the dashboard of his truck, turned the key, and *Taco Wok* burst to life.

"*Fa...ji...tas,*" the ghost uttered.

"Nice to meet you, Fajitas," the woman said, looking at Mr. Anderson as she gunned the truck to life and the trio peeled down the road. "I'm this town's Faust, but you can call me Harley."

The necklace jerked in Axl's hand, nearly loosing itself from the mirror as it bolted. Axl grabbed it and yelped in pain.

"Yeah, I wouldn't touch it," Harley said, looking out the back of the truck at the red light as she sped them along.

"It's jinxed and angry. It wants to reconnect with Rudolph back there."

"If you could make some sense, please," Axl said, holding the mirror further away. "And start by why you boosted my truck—and where are we going? And what is that thing back there?"

Harley jerked the wheel to dodge a slow-moving Chrysler as *Taco Wok* jumped into traffic.

"First, that thing is a catalyst jinn," Harley explained. "What you do is, you separate a piece of the jinn, contain that piece in something," Harley gestured to the pendant, "and then you put an unknowing mark between the jinn and its missing piece. Once they connect—bam—you've just sent some poor bastard to the jinn's home plane. Wrecks holy terror on our psychic plane meanwhile."

Could explain my emotions being so wonky, Axl thought. "So why's it after me?"

70

"It's not," Harley said, turning abruptly through more traffic. "The catalyst jinn was feeding on ghosts to keep up its energy as it sought its missing piece, and Fajitas here was its latest bite until I came on the scene with this pendant. I got tricked. I'm the mark."

Axl was quiet, as was Fajitas.

"Second, that's a '69 SS I'm driving," Harley snickered. "You think I'm going to let the jinn do to my ride what it's done to yours? No sir. Killed me as it was to rip the mirror off.

"And last," Harley said, flooring the gas pedal. She stared into the distance ahead of them, eyes steely. "The pendant was on loan. I plan to return it."

*   *   *   *   *

Mama da Capo napped leisurely, not quite asleep, nor was she awake, existing in a twilight of awareness and dream that she found intoxicating.

71

Nearly the entirety of The Court of Lesser Fiends springing to awareness shook her from her revelry, and she sat bolt upright.

The food truck slowly idled into the alleyway. One could have easily assumed the driver was lost and about to stop and back out. But then it crashed into the wall, scraping to a complete stop less than five yards from Mama's pillow palace.

Danger/Assassin/Beware! Les Enfants warned.

Mama da Capo flicked her finger forward, and two shadows peeled off the walls nearby, slinking toward the truck. The back roof was missing, Mama noticed, as the engine began to smoke. She couldn't see a driver.

One of the shadows heard a noise from inside the truck. A jittering tapping was coming from the glovebox.

Mama saw the red streak bearing down on her alley too late as the shadow opened the glovebox to find Mama's pendant wrapped around a broken rearview mirror. There was a note attached that read *The marker has come collected.*

A deafening roar filled the alleyway as the catalyst jinn collected itself, followed by a blinding red-yellow light and a rush of wind. The Court of Lesser Fiends to a member was gone—even Mama da Capo's bean bags.

No one had a chance to scream.

*　*　*　*　*

Axl looked at *Taco Wok*—or what remained—as Harley checked the alley for Mama or any Court members who avoided getting rehomed.

"You've got insurance, yeah?" Harley asked as she made her way back.

"I do," Axl sighed. "Though, what do I do about him?"

Fajitas milled about the back of the truck, touching the grill top lovingly.

"Nah, don't worry about Fajitas," Harley said. "He's taken a shine to your restaurant, but the party's over. Now that the psychic plane is returning to normal, no one should see him or hear a peep from him anymore. Unless they were already predisposed."

"Maybe I'll go brick-and-mortar," Axl wondered.

"Your call," Harley adjusted her ponytail, pulling some loose red strands back. "But who knows? A ghost might be good for business. Hey, can you give me a ride back to my car?"

*   *   *   *   *

Cliff unlocked the back door to his pizzeria and readied the store for opening, humming *Sympathy For The Devil*. Maybe it was a little on the nose, but it always put a little pep in Cliff's step. Sure, his joint was a front for devilry, but that didn't mean Cliff couldn't take some pride in a job well done.

A flash of heat ran down Cliff's spine as he bent over his last table, wiping it clean. He stood up but didn't turn around.

"Get. Out," Cliff said.

"Now, Cliffy," Harley said, seated in the corner booth. She had her legs drawn up and was playing the drums on her knees. "You're not still upset by my little prank last time, right? I didn't touch the booze! And hey! Look at the pipes on you. Should've known you were a Stones fan."

Cliff sighed a deep, long sigh and then turned around.

"What do you want now, Faust?" Cliff asked. "I'm trying to run a business here!"

Harley hopped up and patted the air with her hands in a *calm-down* motion.

"I know you are, you handsome devil," Harley said, smiling at her joke. "And I won't be two shakes of a lamb's tail. I just wondered: do you have any leads on an original

rearview mirror for the Camaro?"

Mr. Pop Top

Sometimes the guy knew. Sometimes, he didn't.

I can't say what the difference was, what changed about things from one night to the next, but it was our nightly ritual. I'd come out the front door from the apartment complex, headed wherever, and there he'd be, invariably on the stoop, surrounded by empty cans.

"Hey, Mr. Pop Top," that's what I called him. Hell else kinda name should I give him? "Where's she at tonight?"

He'd squint up his eyes real good for a second and, on the nights he knew, say, "Playin' checkers off 7th" or "Singin' Bessie Smith' tover at Sugars." Nights he didn't know, he squinted hard and then just shrugged.

I don't know if he's crazy or what, and I don't know who *She* is. Our routine is the only communication I've ever gotten out of him. He's just a character in my life, doing his thing while I do mine. We're cool with it. I'm not one of those people who need to analyze everything. Sometimes a mystery in your life is a good thing. Not for solving, just to keep things interesting. Lets me know that nobody has all the answers.

But tonight, something set him off in an entirely different direction.

"Yo, Mr. Pop Top, where's she at tonight?"

He stood up in my path.

"I want to come," He said matter-of-factly.

"I, uh, I don't think that's a good idea. I'm going to a club. Ya know? Loud music, dancing, drinking. It's not— I'm just saying, I don't think you'd like it." I dug around in my coat, looking for any reason to break eye contact with him. I found some gum.

"I want to come," he repeated.

I slowly opened a stick of gum and popped it in my mouth.

"Look, hey, you do what you wanna do. You dig clubs, too. Okay, I get it. Alright, I'll—I'm just gonna walk in this general direction," I gestured with a head nod, "and you feel free to come along. Or not. Whatever you want."

We started walking.

Two blocks down, he hadn't turned around, so Mr. Pop Top was coming to a club with me.

"So…are you an R and B guy?" I asked, pushing my hands deeper into my coat pockets, "Or, how about—any hip hop?" He didn't answer. "Probably not. I'm good with all kinds of music, really. Play a little. Keyboard. Mostly Techno." I was running out of small talk. "I was at a rave once a few years back—this was when raves were cool—anyhow, this dude told me that my playing spoke to his colon in waves of neon Kool-Aid. I'm not sure what that meant, but I took it as a compliment."

Mr. Pop Top just walked along beside me, looking down at his feet. We were six or seven blocks from the club.

"Hey, so, who is this *She* that you always talk about?"

No answer. Mr. Pop Top just kept his eyes down.

"I only ask because—"

Suddenly, there were two guys in front of us. One had a gun.

"Money. Now." The gunman said. His buddy took a step toward Mr. Pop Top.

"Hey, easy—" When I tried to get between them, the gunman brought his gun level to my head and slapped me with it. I fell to the ground hard.

The second mugger grabbed Mr. Pop Top by his coat.

"Are you deaf, old man?" he said. "Give us your money." The gunman kept his gun on me.

I'm not sure what happened next. I mean, I *know* what happened; I just don't understand *how* it happened. The gunman's gun kind of…dissolved into his hand, causing him to give the most piercing scream I've ever heard. The smell was worse, believe it or not. He ran back into the alley. The other mugger, who grabbed Mr. Pop Top, he just sort of…flew away. Straight up into the night.

Mr. Pop Top was looking up into the sky after him. I sat on the sidewalk for a few minutes. This kinda thing, you don't—you *can't* just witness and go on your merry way. I had to wrap my head around it. I know, I just got done telling you that sometimes a mystery in your life is a good thing, but I finally asked,

"Mr. Pop Top?" he looked down at me, "Where's she at tonight?"

He looked back up into the night sky.

Smiling.

Thicket Man

Peter came in from his morning run to the sound of a familiar chime emanating from his computer. Wiping the sweat from his brow with the sleeve of his already damp shirt, he hit the keys to answer the call.

Robert's face appeared on the screen; his eyes were narrowed. He gave a heavy sigh.

"Good morning, Bobby," Peter said cheerily. "Hope I haven't kept you waiting."

"Two minutes and counting," Robert gruffed. "Still going out every morning, I see. What exactly does 'stay home' mean to you?"

"It's a wooded path that no one else uses, so a six-foot separation isn't a problem," Peter explained in a way that said it wasn't for the first time.

"Your eyes are baggy," Robert pointed out. "Even through the monitor, I can see you're tired."

Peter rubbed his eyes. The truth was, he hadn't been sleeping well—not for weeks. But he wasn't about to explain to his business partner what was keeping him up at night—nightmares worse than any he'd had as a kid about a monster that was hunting him.

No, there was no way Robert was going to hear about Thicket Man.

"Self-isolation just isn't my thing," Peter offered. "So, let's call this meeting to order, yeah? The merger still looks good to go on the 20th, quarantined or not. Did you line up the transfer of the stocks as I asked?"

"I still think it's a mistake," Robert sighed, looking down at some paperwork on his desk. "But what do I know?"

***

Peter ran.

But no matter how he ran, regardless of which direction, Thicket Man was always right there in the shadows, whispering his rhyme.

"When seventeen does come to pass,

Then none alive can save your ass

For once I've marked, I make my kill

Then sidle up and eat my fill!"

So Peter ran.

But no matter how he ran. . .

***

Peter awoke, screaming, sitting upright in bed.

It was 3:37 in the morning.

He leaned over and turned on the bedside table lamp, then reached for the pad and pencil next to it. He penciled in another mark next to the crossed hatches on the paper.

Seventeen times, he'd had the dream of the Thicket Man.

Seventeen times, he'd died.

84

Today was the day, it seemed. The sweat streaming down Peter's back made his flesh shiver into goose pimples. He told himself it was because he'd forgotten to turn the A.C. up before bed, but knew it was more than that.

"This is ridiculous," Peter thought. "She's gotten into my head."

Peter got out of bed, booted up his laptop, and rang up Tessa.

"Pete," she answered, wearing headphones and a distracted look as her focus was drawn to another monitor. "Can't chat just now. Midquest. You understand."

"Don't hang up!" Peter shouted. "Today's the day. Seventeen times I've dreamt of Thicket Man."

"Need a sec, guys," Tessa quieted her game and finally looked at Peter. "Christ, you look like shit."

"Yeah, well, it's your fault if I do," Peter rubbed his eyes. "Listen, I know I blew off your woo-woo talk before but -"

"Never mind that now," Tessa interrupted. "What you need to do is be very aware of your surroundings. Also, how much salt do you have on hand?"

***

Tessa first came into Peter's life via an online forum about recurring dreams that Peter had, early on in the story of Thicket Man, stumbled upon as he was searching for any avenue he could find to make sense of everything. She talked of nightmares that served as premonitions, how to ward off danger, and spells one could use in self-preservation.

Which were the very kinds of comments that decided Peter on avoiding contact with her.

Until Day 17.

"Make a circle out of salt, check. Cover all reflective surfaces, check." Peter went down the list Tessa had provided. It was four in the afternoon, so sleep deprivation made it all seem less wacky.

Peter didn't own a shotgun, let alone any rock salt to load it with, and he and Tessa decided that the less he left the house, the better.

So, with the list completed otherwise, Peter sat down inside the circle. He had a tablet and a broom to which he'd duct-taped a steak knife. A makeshift spear, Tessa had told him, was better than nothing.

He proceeded to read the book he'd downloaded, *Cryptozoology: What We Don't Know Is Out There,* but kept a wary eye on the rest of his living room, too, jumping at shadows that danced across his furniture as the sun began to set.

***

Peter woke to the chiming of his laptop from the office. He'd fallen asleep at some point in the night and landed in a faceful of salt. Spitting out his protection, Peter got up and groggily made his way to his desk.

"Yeah," he said to the blurry face on his monitor.

"Good lord, man," Robert gasped. "You look like you slept in your car."

"Not far off," Peter sat down hard in his chair. "What's up?"

"Not much. I just wanted to check in with you before this conference call with New York," Robert said, shuffling some papers. "We're three days out from done, partner."

Peter grunted in response. Stupid Tessa and her dumb mumbo-jumbo.

"Go get your run in," Robert laughed. "I'll call back the moment I'm off with New York."

***

Peter started to feel better about everything around a quarter-mile into his run.

So he'd entertained a small flight of fancy. Who had it hurt, really? He hadn't had the dream last night, so everything was okay now. He was probably just working too hard. If nothing else, he had an entertaining story to tell at parties. It all came down to stress. But he'd be able to relax for a bit as soon as the merger was over, maybe even take a vacation. Like Robert had said, only three more days.

As Peter followed the turn in the path, a random thing occurred to him. He hadn't followed up with Robert about his lining up the stock; hadn't checked that it was done. What if Robert sold the stock without telling him? It would make for a tidy sum of money.

The trail naturally curled, courtesy of deer—the trailblazers of Peter's exercise routine—avoiding a small grove of trees.

A thicket.

Peter began to slow his run as a strange clarity hit him, causing many things to click in his mind at once, some fifty yards from the trees.

First, there was movement coming from within the thicket.

Secondly, today's date was the seventeenth.

Third, Robert knew how much it cost to kill someone.

And finally, though she'd gotten the details wrong, Tessa had been right after all.

Everything ended with a barely perceptible *Pop*.

Parker Klumpett's Antique Refrigerator

The air conditioning wasn't working. That's important to understand going into this. That one little fact colors everything else you're about to discover.

Parker Klumpett stood in front of his 1949 Sears Coldspot refrigerator, hoping to find a respite from the heat, but he came up empty. Even as he leaned in front of the open fridge, his shirt began to soak through with sweat. Perspiration ran in small rivers from his brow, down his nose, and onto the floor.

Some people can handle the heat—that suffocating feeling of breathing in hot air that makes your lungs feel like warm, wet towels, but Parker couldn't count himself among them. His body reacted to the increasing temperature, in part, through acute clarity of his mind's eye.

For instance, the Crawford boy was mowing somebody's lawn outside. His mower needed a new engine, so it ran rough and smoked while circling around trees and lawn features. Also, hornets were attempting to build a nest just inside the rarely used side door into Parker's house, as evidenced by the faint buzzing Parker could hear.

No, nothing got past Parker Klumpett's senses while he was heat-raging.

This is why he immediately noticed the sound of his refrigerator's motor going from gentle hum to dzzzz, to ka-thunk, ka-thunk, to dead.

"Not you, too!" Parker yelled. He shut the door to the Coldspot and dropped to his knees in front of it, hoping against hope that his actions might restart the motor.

They did not.

Parker, cursing, slid around to the back of the Coldspot in a futile effort—since he knew nothing about antique refrigerator maintenance—to see what made the motor stop.

As his eyes slid over the cover to the motor, the world suddenly went upside-down and inside-out.

An astoundingly loud F note—possibly from a bassoon?—brought Parker awake, followed by a blindingly bright, intense green. Just the color, BAM!, in his face.

Shaking it off, he found himself in what appeared to be the storage space (he was housed between a box of fireplace billows and two 10-speed bikes) of something that was moving.

He tried to stand up, but another bass note from some other kind of wind instrument played at him again, followed by a shock of teal overwhelming his vision in what Parker had to admit was an effective one-two punch.

"What is this!?" Parker yelled.

"Ah, ThErE wE gO," a voice rose, seemingly from the room itself, in shifting tones. "i'Ve BeEn TrYiNg To GeT a ReAcTiOn FoR /::/TIME CONSTRUCT DEFINITION UNFAMILIAR/::/."

"What is—who is talk—where am I?" Parker gasped, trying to take in his surroundings, locate the disembodied voice, and stand up at the same time. Another bout of vertigo, as though the room he was in was falling fast, shooting backward, and veering left all at once, hit him then. Parker sat back down hard, closed his eyes, and tried his very best not to vomit.

"fAsCiNaTiNg," the voice began again. "UtIlIzInG a CoRpOrEaL oRgAn To CoMmUnIcAte. HoW vErY pRiMiTiVe."

"Can you please," Parker belched his stomach's distress, almost coming in loaded, "not talk like that. The pitching octaves are making this," another near-fire burp, "even harder to take."

Parker opened his eyes again and found that he had, at some point during this ordeal, lain down on the floor. He began to focus on words printed on the ceiling:

MREUS WAAAA

"I apologize," the voice returned, more even this time. "It has been a challenge, finding the correct wavelengths in which to observe you best, let alone communicate properly."

"Well, that's much easier on me, thank you," Parker said. The world seemed to run in a straight line momentarily, so Parker took the opportunity to get to his feet. Or at least that had been his intent. His surroundings became that of an infinite cosmos of melting colors and shifting light, causing him to stumble, falling through space not beholden to the laws of physics as he understood them.

"Apologies again," the voice said. Parker looked up from underneath his arms, tucked away in a protective ball as he was. He was once more indoors. "I was distracted by the charm and strange flavours."

Parker reburied his face under his arms. When he braved one eye open, trying to ensure that he was, in fact, inside a ship of some sort, he locked onto the motor cover to his refrigerator. It seemed to be attached to a meshwork of odds and ends hanging from the wall.

"My . . . that's my . . . ," Parker stammered.

"Oh, yes," the voice continued. "Motor components from a 1949 Coldspot were necessary for, well, here. See for yourself."

The inside of the room pitched left-up and then dissolved into a series of black and white dots, digitizing his reality in a way that made Parker briefly reflect on the 8-bit video games of his youth. Then came sounds like he was underwater, and something was rushing by very quickly, followed by socks. Just a sea of socks, varying in color and size with nary a one matching, as far as Parker could see. Then his senses expanded, accepting data through every nerve-ending in ways that this, his host body, had never experienced before. Beyond pain, pleasure, into the abstract so profoundly, it was equally exhilarating and horrifying.

"Yes, ahem," the voice, sounding distracted, came again. "You're a slippery one. I'll be throwing you back now. I think, yes, this will do."

When Parker's awareness returned, he found himself aboard a train. The countryside whirling past outside his compartment window was completely foreign to him, as was any recollection of how he had arrived inside a speeding train.

"Hmm. Snow-topped mountains," Parker noted, the dichotomy of a calm reaction externally, while inwardly his head was spinning. "Well, at least it's not hot here."

Road Rage

"Big storm, coming in from the south," the radio host explained in his hip, cool-guy voice. "We're talking R-A-I-N!"

The two vehicles sped, weaving around their fellow road warriors like angry bees. The green truck was powerful— mighty—with a fearsome tiger painted on its hood. The beast roared, alive, as the engine revved, barreling down the highway after the little silver Hyundai.

The smaller car was being driven by a man named Martin, who honestly didn't know what he could have possibly done to warrant such a reaction from the truck's sole occupant, but he wasn't about to heed the man's shouted suggestion to "pull over!" That seemed counterproductive to Martin's continued breathing.

The rabbit tattoo on his wrist peeked out from under his suit jacket as he slammed the steering wheel first left, then right, dodging a Dodge Ram truck. Martin didn't miss the irony.

The truck came around the front of the Dodge, nearly clipping it as it jumped in behind Martin. Martin braced for the hit as the tiger filled up his rearview mirror, but it didn't come. Not yet, anyway. Martin spun his Hyundai to the right, driving on the side of the highway.

The truck followed, closing in again.

The Check Engine light came on just under Martin's GPS; his car's way of letting him know that he'd better think of something quick, or they were both screwed.

Martin scanned the road in front of him, his eyes darting back and forth from the metal monster that was giving such good chase behind. He looked to the GPS to try and glean what, if anything, was coming. It just showed a long stretch of desert highway devoid of any help. Why couldn't the Highway Patrol show up right now? He'd call them himself if his cell wasn't dead. The Hyundai wasn't going to last much longer, he knew. Exceeding 100 mph for this long was not something it was prepared for, what with so much time having passed between maintenance checks.

"Think, Martin. Think." He muttered to himself. He looked over at the wall of dark clouds moving toward them from the south. Like an evil blanket sent to snuff them out.

The truck roared again behind him, twenty feet, then ten, then five. He was going to hit Martin this time. Ram him off the road. But then he didn't, again. The truck dropped back some four car lengths. Lightning split the air above them at nearly the exact moment that the thunder boomed. The highway had emptied, save for the two of them, as Mother Nature provided her very own end-of-the-world soundtrack. The rain came down thick like a river falling from the sky. Both Martin and the insane truck driver turned their headlights on.

"Surely, now we can be done," Martin said to the rearview mirror version of the madman in the truck. He dropped down to 75 mph, but the tiger started to pounce behind him, so he kicked it back up to 90 mph. But Martin did notice that the truck seemed warier—maybe less inclined to go all out under the deluge that was trying to drown them.

This gave Martin an idea.

He swerved into the left lane of the highway, and the truck followed carefully. He coasted back over to the right side, and the truck stayed with him, but haltingly. Martin realized then that the truck's driver was having a hard time making out Martin's silver Hyundai in all of this rain. He was probably only following Martin's taillights.

Martin looked back at his GPS. He scrolled the map on the screen up some to find what he was looking for. Finally, he saw it—a giant bend in the highway, not six miles ahead.

Martin pulled back into the left side lane of the highway. The truck did, too. Martin sped up. The truck followed. Faster they went. 80. 85. The rain was pelting Martin's windshield. Visibility consisted of nothing but water burying his windshield wipers. He gave up and used the GPS to navigate. 90. 95. The truck's engine gunned behind him, its headlights filling the Hyundai with dull yellow light. The hit was coming, but so was the curve in the road.

Then Martin cut off his headlights and spun his car into the curve without braking.

With no visibility of its own and seemingly no GPS, the truck slammed on its brakes once Martin effectively went invisible, but it was going far too fast to avoid what was happening. It careened off the highway, flipping as it left the pavement, and rolled into the desert at 100 miles per hour.

Martin turned his headlights back on and slowed down to a more sensible 40 mph, given the weather conditions.

His Check Engine light went back off.

To Ponder

Harper played with the wad of putty, absently rolling it around on her desk as she ignored her work, the cursor blinking on the screen at the end of her unfinished sentence. Having honed the talent of zoning out to an art form while she was at M.I.T., Harper could put her body on autopilot and just send her mind away.

Her Pop called it Delving.

It wasn't Zen. She wasn't emptying her mind or intensely focusing on a single flame, nothing like that. It wasn't even peaceful blankness. No, when Harper delved, she focused on the Plan.

Harper had been an eight-year-old kid, flying alone on a 747 from her Mom's place in California back to her Pop's in Michigan when she first started to develop the Plan. It was late evening, just before the inky black of night. Harper could still make out the dark purple/blue of a day that didn't want to let go as she looked out the plane's window to the horizon. It had been cloudy. Her California trip had gone two days longer than it should have, in her opinion, and she was ready to be home in Michigan with her Pop. The flight attendant had a warm, friendly smile and had given Harper an extra bag of peanuts.

She was just about to fall asleep when the murmuring started.

All around Harper, other passengers were talking amongst themselves and looking out the windows of the plane into the night sky. Some pointed. Others laughed nervously. One young boy got frantic and had to be shushed by an old man he was traveling with, all due to something outside of the plane.

Harper looked out of her window.

A light shone from inside the clouds, rotating in amber, green, and white, like a confused lighthouse, as it matched the jet's speed. It was the most beautiful thing Harper had

ever seen. She felt no fear as she watched it speed up and

slow down out in the night. For ten whole minutes, the light

followed Harper's 747. Then, as suddenly as it had

appeared, it shot straight up and disappeared.

It was right then that Harper slipped into herself,

delving into the quiet of her mind, and began the initial

stage of what had become the Plan.

She had told her Pop about the lights, of course, it was

too fantastic an event not to. He had shared in her

enthusiasm when he heard the tale, and the two of them had

visited the library the next day to research anything they

could find about lights in the sky and UFOs.

"The path to every answer has its start in a book

somewhere." Her Pop had told her, "Reading tunes your

mind; opens it. Enables you to take whatever you're feeling

and focus it into ideas; into thoughts that can let you make sense of things."

But Harper didn't tell him about The Plan. At eight years old, she didn't know the words to describe it. Even at twenty-eight, after graduating from M.I.T. and starting her own software company, Harper still didn't know how to explain The Plan to anyone.

Partially because the blueprint that was The Plan was always evolving. It began with amber, green, and white. That was the template. But then, when Harper went to the library with her Pop, it changed. The feeling that came from learning beside her father was added to the colors, and joy became part of The Plan. As she aged, The Plan gained depth, substance even, but it was ever incomplete. Like trying to put together a jigsaw puzzle with no picture to go by, using pieces you only discovered throughout the day-to-day living of life. Each time Harper found a potential new piece, she would delve—go to her quiet place, the one that belonged entirely to The Plan—and try and place it there.

The first time she had sex, the mathematical formula that is Chopin's Nocturne in C-sharp minor, the technology involved in an iPad's touch screen, the nervous system of an arthropod, all of these things and so much more made up The Plan's structure. Nonsensical arrangements when splayed out in words, but poetry in the context and confines of Harper's delving place. An insular notion, desperately wishing to dwell with stars.

Today Harper was delving after having learned a new word. *Bagicha*, Hindi for garden. Hearing it had struck that familiar chord within her, particularly once she blended its pronunciation with her memory of what black licorice tasted like. She began to roll the wad of putty counterclockwise.

Something in Harper's mind opened further. She rose above The Plan, first as herself—as Harper—then as Harper-That-Was. She stretched, simultaneously rising higher and falling lower while her sense of self merely… expanded. Realizing with equal clarity all that is Harper, as Harper pertained to the wad of putty pertained to the IKEA desk, pertained to the building's electrical system, to Detroit, to steel, soil, rock, magma, satellite, nebulae, hydrogen, fission, 193472047603294752

"Harper?" a voice said, "Harper! Are you okay?"

"I—" Harper blinked her eyes a few times and moved her head from side to side before looking at her head researcher. "Yeah, I'm good. What's up?"

"You looked, I dunno, elsewhere." He made his way over from the door to Harper's office to look more closely at her. "I said your name like four times."

"Yeah," Harper sighed, "I had something on my mind."

The Scorpion and the Crow

It is an age of wonder.

Monsters and magic run as commonplace as swords and shields, and the coin of the realm is adventure.

But superstition is its lifeblood.

A babe born into this world imperfect was often cast out as impure, as touched by evil, demonic. Left to the providence of the elements, or, for the immoral, money-minded parents, sold to those with dark intentions.

Such was the fate of the denizens of Tangleknot Cave.

*　*　*

"Orynthesca is bitter today," Tess mumbled, taking care not to nick herself as her pale, nimble fingers sliced blue fungus loose from the cavern wall. A small crow tattoo lived on her left hand, on the web of flesh between her finger and thumb.

Collecting the fungus as well, Mu'dai gave a noncommittal nod. As this was the young girl's typical response, Tess didn't even bother looking for confirmation in the torchlight the two shared.

"Mu'dai...do you ever think about leaving? What you'll do once your days are your own?" Tess wondered to her friend, her sister, without looking up from her work.

Mu'dai paused, holding the blue fungus she'd freed from the wall above their basket, and stared up at Tess. The girl was a mirror image of Mu'dai. Pale-skinned where Mu'dai was dark, sure, and Mu'dai's similarly placed tattoo was a scorpion, not a crow, but it went beyond this. Orynthesca had collected Tess for being born blind in her right eye. Mu'dai wasn't blind, but she had a dark patch of skin—a birthmark in the shape of a handprint—that covered her left eye and ran up her scalp, turning her raven hair stark white in four distinctive streaks. Having only vague recollections of their families before Tangleknot Cave, the two would sometimes pretend to be twins, split at birth.

One soul in two bodies.

Truth be told, Mu'dai never thought about leaving Tangleknot Cave beyond the necessary hunting for food and the collection of winter provisions for the cave. This was her life, and she was adept at living it. But, of course, Spyders—what Orynthesca referred to her reclaimed children as—*did* leave. They aged beyond what the witch found useful and eventually made their way into the world.

"Never mind, sister," Tess said, misunderstanding Mu'dai's silence. "I was just—"

"Winky, Mud Eye, snap to," a deep voice bellowed from outside their cavern. "It's showtime. Best not keep the mistress waiting."

A twisted soul hidden under layers of fat, Dorner was Orynthesca's right-hand man and the only other adult to walk the caverns of Tangleknot. He was her eyes and ears outside of the cave, as Orynthesca only left on the rare occasion to collect another Spyder.

Tess gathered up the basket, placing her slender blade inside, while Mu'dai removed their torch from the rocks, and both girls began the trip back to Orynthesca in the Great Hall of the main cavern. They walked past Dorner with their eyes down, as dutiful Spyders learned to do.

"Wait now," Dorner barked, grabbing hold of Tess's arm. "I must say, Winky, you're growing into quite a looker. Ya know, so long as you keep that freakish eye toward the wall. Hey, now, why don't you hang back?"

Tess's eyes went wide and unfocused yet remained downturned.

"Only for a few minutes!" Dorner sneered what he seemingly thought was a reassuring smile. The oil from his thin mustache reflected the torchlight. He ran his hand down her arm to the edge of her sheer, dirty dress, pulling at it. "Mistress won't mind. I have something I want to show you."

Mu'dai, who had taken three steps more as Dorner stopped Tess, now turned around.

"Eh, what?" Dorner grunted, sensing Mu'dai's presence and half-turning to look at her behind him. "No, carry on, Mud Eye. You're all spindly arms and legs, next to no curves. Built like a boy, really, wearing trousers and all. You wouldn't appreciate what I've got for our Winky here."

Mu'dai had the torch in one hand and her own slender blade in the other. Opting at that moment for the former, Mu'dai took one step toward Dorner and reached out with the torch.

Smoke began to rise toward the top of the tunnel from where she had lit Dorner on fire.

"Ow!" Dorner spun away from Tess, batting at his shoulder where his singed cloak had begun to flame. "Mule-headed ass!" He swung a free fist toward Mu'dai, who easily dodged. He didn't notice the blade in her other hand as she deftly spun it, prepared to strike. In the chaos, Tess snapped out of her trance.

"*When the Widow summons, her Spyders obey*," Tess half-shrieked as she grabbed Mu'dai, pushing the pair down the tunnel away from the smoking fat man. Mu'dai initially fought against her momentum but quickly allowed Tess to take the lead, tucking the small blade into her belt.

"Time's up, girlies! Just ye wait! Once your fates find ye, what ol' Dorner's offerin' won't seem so bad!" Both girls could hear Dorner yelling down the cavern as they quickly made their way through multiple slender, rocky tunnels. Tess suddenly grabbed the torch from Mu'dai and flung it down a separate shaft before leading the two down another.

"What were you thinking?" Tess hissed, pulling them down to a crouch in the pitch black tunnel. "You were going to kill him—I saw it!"

Mu'dai stiffened at the sound of their approaching pursuer, but the dimwitted Dorner fell for Tess's ruse and chased down the shaft housing their forgotten torch. Mu'dai returned to a standing position, jerking free from Tess as she did so.

"I'll thank you not to read my fate, *sister*," Mu'dai huffed before continuing down the darkened cavern.

"You know I don't have that kind of control," Tess said, then lowered her voice. "I can't help that—"

To my sanctum, at once!

The voice itched, echoing in the minds of both girls in a harsh cacophony of intelligible whispers—its message stretching beyond the capacity of either girl's senses to perceive anything else.

When the Widow of Tangleknot Cave summoned, her Spyders obeyed.

*   *   *

An acrid scent carried within faint wisps of smoke began to emerge, as if fog from the rock walls, as the Spyders filed through the tunnels toward the central cavern of Tangleknot. The smell haunted them, only growing worse—the stench more pungent and the smoke denser—as they neared their mistress.

Mu'dai and Tess saw they were the last to arrive as they entered the gigantic cavern serving as the Great Hall of Tangleknot. Oil-filled braziers burned along the walls, lighting the scene in heat and flame. Orynthesca stood on a small dais carved from a massive stone in the hall's center. Her tall, thin frame stood nude but for her amaranthine orb, ever-present around her neck, and the gilding done by the hands of young children surrounding her. A half-dozen of the younger Spyders, the Hatchlings, covered the witch's body with ornate symbols and patterns as the youngest Spyders, Foundlings, sat in a circle around the dais chanting in hivemind Orynthesca's words.

Brought forth on cosmic winds,

The yawning abyss does near

To claim the cask of darkness,

And banish those who dwell

In the False Lord's light

A slight shiver ran up Mu'dai's back at the sound of the small children, mere toddlers, chanting Chigauroth's prayer. Being part of the hivemind was always harsher for Mu'dai than it had been for the other children when she

119

was their age. All Spyders shared the same childhood—tattooed with various animals as Foundlings, taught to paint the correct symbols as Hatchlings—but unlike the others, Mu'dai's wits always remained during the intonement, as though Mu'dai wandered lost in a dream behind the words, separating herself from her mistress's mind.

Orynthesca never warmed to this fact.

"You Who Are Less stand judged before Chigauroth and found wanting," the witch said, her booming voice echoing throughout the cavern. The Hatchlings, having completed placing the necessary symbols on Orythnesca's body, sat on the cavern floor next to the Foundlings as the toddlers continued to chant quietly. Finally, she turned a tilted head toward Mu'dai and Tess. *Crow. Scorpion. To your places.*

The itchy-brain feeling overcame both girls again as their mistress silently spoke to them directly. As the eldest

Spyders, Tess and Mu'dai had places of prestige in the Great Hall during a calling ritual. Essentially, they were to stand upon their prepared sigils at opposite ends of the hall to better channel Orynthesca's power as the witch called upon Chigauroth for enlightenment.

Tonight would be the third time she and Tess stood in the prestigious spaces, and, as far as Mu'dai knew, Chigauroth had never shown enlightenment to their mistress on the other occasions.

In unison born of repeated performances, both girls climbed the stone steps that marked the narrow path up to their positions. Mu'dai's eyes began to wet from the scent and smoke that filled the cavern as she climbed, one heavy foot in front of the other, until she reached her mark, the sigil of a scorpion carved into the rock. Then, turning, she found herself still in concert with Tess, with the girls now facing each other. Once everyone was in position, the ceremony began as it always did. The Hatchlings joined the

Foundlings' hivemind, chanting:

Brought forth on cosmic winds,

The yawning abyss does near

To claim the cask of darkness,

And banish those who dwell

In the False Lord's light

Then, at a certain point—at the exact moment in every

ceremony—Orynthesca screamed, a bloodcurdling shriek

echoing along the walls amidst the smoke and stench.

Something was different this time, Mu'dai noticed.

There were voices within the echoes of the witch's scream,

buried at its edges. Whispered secrets of bloodletting and

flesh consumed by moldy time. Mu'dai saw then—painted

in the hushed murmurs—visions of discarded Spyders,

mere husks, their meat gone bad through holes in the

bodies, dashed skulls, and broken bones, all dumped unceremoniously within a secret cavern in Tangleknot.

Not freed upon a wide world at a certain age, but fed to a dark, lonesome cave.

Then this was not a call for enlightenment to some lost elder god across the cosmos, Mu'dai realized, but a dinner bell to feed something ancient closer to home.

And with that realization came a voice she recognized, deep within the cacophony of dark muttering.

Something wrong is going to happen! Tess's voice yelled just behind Mu'dai's consciousness, causing her to jump. **We've got to stop her!**

Mu'dai attempted to shake off the smoke's effects as best she could, but it was hard to do, as high as she was in the cavern. She knelt, gasping for cleaner air. Then, shaking her head free of the horrifying vision, Mu'dai began to crawl down the steps from her stony plinth. Though the thickening smoke made it increasingly difficult, she could see the outline of Tess across the cavern, still standing at her perch.

I ca—move—legs. Tess's voice raced across Mu'dai's brain in broken jumbles, lost amidst the sea of other angrier whispers. The smoke seeping from the cavern walls grew thicker as Mu'dai continued crawling down the stone stairs. The accompanying sour scent became ever stronger. Finally, she tumbled down the last few and stood shakily, untrusting of her own legs.

"Tess?" Mu'dai managed to croak, her throat growing raw from breathing the accursed air. A dark wind kicked up, swirling the thick smoke. She made her way toward her sister, stumbling through the maelstrom as though one blind as the chanting ebbed and flowed in volume over the dark-spirited whispers and bleak portents.

Brought forth on cosmic winds,

The yawning abyss does near

To claim the cask of darkness,

And banish those who dwell

In the False Lord's light

Mu'dai crossed the length of the hall toward Tess's raised position, but as she grew closer to Orynthesca's shrine, her sibling Spyders' chants growing louder in the dark, the witch's arm shot out from the smoke and pulled Mu'dai up off the ground and toward her nightmarish visage. The flesh of Orynthesca's face swirled as one with the smoke whirling around the hall, its features dancing as maiden, mother, and crone in turn. Her eye bulged and sagged with age as her lips pouted pink and beautiful, then jagged slashes wiped the work away as though the details were but done in charcoal on a child's parchment and begun anew.

You, the witch's voice screeched around and through Mu'dai's mind.

Mu'dai flinched, pulling back against Orynthesca's hold, but gained no ground. Then the young girl grasped the knife at her belt and quickly slashed the hand that held her, causing the Widow of Tangleknot Cave to drop her prey. Mu'dai took in then, standing stark against the grimness of the cave, the monstrous new form—or maybe it was her actual shape, Mu'dai quickly wondered—of Orynthesca. Beneath her painted upper torso, with its transforming face and customary arms and hands, was attached the translucent body of a cavern crayfish. Mu'dai nearly met her end as the crayfish's pincers click-clacked at her face, snapping her out of her astonished stare.

"Dorner!" the witch turned her head and yelled, the orb glowing a deep purple at her neck. "Finish the ritual! We must nourish our Lord!"

Mu'dai slunk into the smoke as the wind and the chanting grew ever louder, sneaking behind a thick stalagmite toward Tess. Her mind's voice was the only clarity Mu'dai could find as she crept.

Tess? she thought, nearly picturing each letter in the name individually for emphasis.

I can't seem…it. Tess's voice was dimming under the madness of the cavern hall. Then, ever so faintly,

Something has me, Mu'dai.

"No!" Mu'dai stood, and it saved her life as the crayfish claw smashed into the stalagmite she'd been hiding behind, obliterating the stony deposits.

You Who Are Less stand judged before Chigauroth, and I'll drag you to our Lord's stomach myself! The creature that had been Orynthesca bellowed with a force that seemed to shake Mu'dai's brain.

Mu'dai rolled away from the second claw attack, narrowly dodging a seated Spyder— she could no longer tell Foundling from Hatchling as all of the smaller children's eyes had gone white as they continued chanting over the smoky storm.

Brought forth on cosmic winds,

The yawning abyss does near

To claim the cask of darkness,

And banish those who dwell

In the False Lord's light

Sister...hurry, came Tess, her voice now a whisper in Mu'dai's mind.

Mu'dai dove through the smoke, her small knife still in hand, toward where she thought the path to Tess was, feeling the rush of Orynthesca's movements behind her. Luckily, the first stone step was before her. She started the climb, walking sideways with her blade drawn in her right hand—toward Orynthesca's direction—though aware that Dorner, too, might be in the direction she was heading. Mu'dai stepped lightly but quickly up the stone steps, one by one, as they became visible in front of her.

Mu'dai heard a clicking even over the din of the roaring wind within Tangleknot. She thought at first, as she made her way forward, that it was Orynthesca's crayfish form making its way up the stairs behind her, but the sound came from in front of her.

A deep rumbling belched throughout the cavern as the stone staircase began to tremble underneath Mu'dai. Stumbling about to keep her balance, she knelt, nearly crawling, and continued up the stairs. She placed her small dagger in her mouth to free up both hands, skittering up the carved rock on the tips of her fingers and toes.

Luckily, Mu'dai dared a look back in time to see Orynthesca, unable in her new form to navigate the path after Mu'dai, snap a stalagmite from the ground, and fling it up after her prey. Mu'dai rolled, dangling off the edge of the stairs as solid rock shot over where she'd been but a heart's beat before.

Orynthesca roared in frustration as Mu'dai, pulling herself upright, continued after Tess up the stairs. The air grew increasingly thicker with smoke and stench, causing Mu'dai to cough and retch as her stomach heaved. Soon the steps in front of her were no longer visible, yet higher she climbed, dagger back in hand.

"I should have reached Tess by now," Mu'dai noticed.

She cried out with her thoughts again, yet the sound of the wind was the only response. Then, finally, Mu'dai came to Tess's sigil, a crow. It glowed blue-white in the darkening cavern, yet Tess was not there.

"Tess!" she screamed.

Ever so briefly, the smoke parted enough that Mu'dai could make out a space in the wall beyond. An emptiness that had never been there; she would have seen it before. Yet, somehow, a passageway had formed. Mu'dai approached it warily, her dagger pointed into the darkness. At its archway, she met a slimy membrane, thick yet transparent, that gave a subtle resistance before her blade sliced through it. Fresh air rushed past her face as though the tunnel had exhaled. Mu'dai paused to breathe it in, trying not to cough, then wiped tears from her smoke-filled eyes and continued down the tunnel.

*   *   *

"It's a damn shame, is what it is," Dorner huffed as he lit the candles around the altar where Tess's catatonic body lay. After lighting the last candle—it had to be nine to keep her under—the flabby man paused to stare at Tess. His hand slid under his trousers to adjust himself.

"Well, now," he snickered. "Nothing saying she's got to be dressed for the ritual."

Dorner moved closer to Tess's upper body, his belly plopping onto her bare arm as he made to pull her dress down. He slid the worn fabric off each of the sleeping girl's shoulders, changed his mind, then grabbed the large dagger from his belt to cut the dress from her.

"Move away, or I will kill you," Mu'dai's voice came from the darkness behind him.

Dorner slowly turned toward the thin girl, still armed with his dagger. He eyed hers as she stepped into the light.

"You gonna kill me, eh? That's a laugh, that is. What, with that pig sticker?"

"Yes," Mu'dai said, stalking forward.

Dorner paused, licking his lips, and wiped the sweat from his brow with his empty hand.

"Mistress is going to be upset that you're botching the ceremony," he said, licking his lips again.

"Orynthesca isn't here," Mu'dai spoke quietly, yet forcefully. "Move away."

Dorner felt a flash of rage at the insolence of this welp and dove at her, slashing his blade. Mu'dai pivoted out of his reach with ease, expecting such an apparent attack. She responded with two quick slashes, one at his dagger hand and its sister at his face. Dorner's dagger dropped to the ground as he put both hands on the gash on his cheek.

He pulled his hand away, covered in blood.

Bellowing, mad with hatred, Dorner made to tackle Mu'dai but gained no ground as she rolled under his arms. The fat man couldn't stop his formidable girth in time, knocking over two of the candles in his wake.

Mu'dai took the opportunity to check if Tess was alive.

Tess? she thought. **Tess, please wake up.**

Mu'dai looked up just in time to slide out of another one of Dorner's tackles, slashing him across the armpit as he flew by. Three more candles fell.

And then it seemed as though the entire world began to shake.

The quake knocked Mu'dai to the ground, and she lost her dagger. Somehow, Dorner was upon her in the chaos. He pinned her shoulders with his massive, meaty hands and slid them to her neck. His fat tongue shot about his mouth as though trying to escape from the exertion of strangling her.

"Kill you, kill you, kill—"

Suddenly, Dorner's eyes began to cross as his tongue turned thinner. And silver. Blood poured from his mouth, covering Mu'dai in gore as Tess removed his dagger from the back of his head.

"I'm sorry!" Tess squealed as Mu'dai crawled out from under the dead Dorner.

"Don't worry about—" Mu'dai had started to say before Tangleknot shook again, this time deeper and longer.

"Let's get out of here," both girls said, getting to their feet.

*   *   *

Their way was dark and full of screams.

All the braziers had gone out in the Great Hall as Mu'dai led Tess back down the stairs from the hidden altar room. Each girl was armed with a blade, though neither could see it in their hand. Mu'dai didn't know if the wind had died down or if the screams were just that much louder.

Once the girls hit the bottom of the stairs, the rocky cavern floor began to squelch with each step they took.

"This—what is happening?" Tess yelled.

I don't know, Mu'dai thought to her. **But it's getting stickier**.

Then came the familiar click-clack, directionless, from somewhere in the abyss around them.

Before Mu'dai could inform Tess that Orthynesca, the Widow of Tangleknot Cave, was now some sort of hybrid monstrosity, the Great Hall filled with intense light as every brazier exploded with ten-foot flame.

And the source of the screaming then became evident.

Orynthesca haphazardly danced around in her crayfish form, pouncing upon Spyders as she caught them two, three at a time. She was pinning them to the floor and, with the orb pendant held above her head, morphing their flesh into the cavern, spreading them like jelly over toast into individual meat rugs.

"Our Lord must feed," *eat his fill of the unworthy*! she kept on, vacillating between screaming aloud and doing so psychically, all to sounds of children—no longer in hivemind—yet still crying in anguished chorus.

Stop!

For an instant, everyone in the Great Hall froze. It took Mu'dai a moment to realize that Tess had been the cause, and just as she did, another massive quake began to hit.

Tess ran toward the monster that was Orynthesca just as the crayfish Widow lunged toward her, then the entirety of Tangleknot upended.

Mu'dai, along with a handful of other Spyders, slid down the floor—as it turned into a wall—dodging stalagmites the best she could as she fell. Eventually, her hip clipped painfully into a large stone, spinning Mu'dai down and further away from where Tess was grappling Orynthesca, but allowing her body to rest in the curve of another stone.

"Our Lord has feasted this day!" Orynthesca screamed in Tess's face as the two played tug-of-war with the purple orb. "And HE HAS RISEN!"

Tess said nothing as she fought for the necklace, her face grim with determination. She'd lost her dagger in the turmoil of the cavern *waking*, so all she could do was claw at the witch's eyes with her free hand as the two danced upon the plinth, pivoting in time with the cavern's rotation. The crayfish's pincers snapped for her legs but only caught Tess's dress's hem for its efforts. Tess noticed the orb briefly as they fought, realizing it had a crayfish inside that matched the tattoo on Orynthesca's hand.

In Tess's lapse in attention, Orynthesca's teeth found her fingers. Tess let out a howl as she lost two, the pinky and ring finger of her left hand, to the Widow's maw.

Mu'dai climbed as fast as she could toward the pair, hurried by her sister's cry.

Foolish girl, Orynthesca's voice snarled in and out of Tess's mind. "I am the Widow of Tangleknot," *possessor of the spherule!* "All will cower when I'm by my Lord Chigauroth's side!"

"It's more like his ribcage!" Mu'dai shouted, diving from behind the pair as they wrestled, landing on Orynthesca's back. She carved her small blade into the wrist of the witch, nearly hacking it off in one go. Tess took the opportunity to wrench the orb free from the Widow's ruined hand.

Upon losing the orb, Orynthesca's face began to sink into itself. Her crayfish form slowly turned into ash.

"M-m-ma-mu" she mouthed as her lower jaw folded into her mouth, her eyes wide in panic.

Mu'dai and Tess each kicked her and watched as her tattered form fell into the depths of her god.

More of the stone cavern turned to flesh as their surroundings shook. Tess held the orb up as she'd seen Orynthesca do. Mu'dai watched as the crayfish inside transformed into the crow tattoo on Tess' mangled hand.

"You're not going to turn into a big crow now that you've got that thing, are you?" Mu'dai worried.

"Gods, I hope not," Tess replied. She was focused hard on something else, though.

"Tess, we've got to get out of here," Mu'dai pleaded.

Tess looked at her sister, her eyes welling with tears. "You're right. Let's go!"

They climbed down, hopping from stalagmite to rocky mound when they could control their exit, sliding at stretches when they couldn't. Finally, Mu'dai saw the light from outside of Tangleknot. She took Tess's hand, and the two slid-fell down what had once been the ceiling to the cave's entrance. Mu'dai looked out at ground that had replaced a horizon.

"We're really inside a standing god," Mu'dai remarked, gobsmacked. "I don't recognize anything about this landscape."

"Chigauroth is teleporting all over the planet," Tess explained. "Until he sleeps, it won't stop."

"It's not far to the ground, though," Mu'dai said, ignoring her. "The fall won't hurt. Much. And we'll figure out where we are. I can hunt anywhere, or we can find work. If there's a city nearby."

Mu'dai, Tess spoke quietly in her mind.

Mu'dai turned, her adrenaline spike growing sour in her veins as she looked into Tess's eyes.

"I can't go," Tess looked down, unable to keep eye contact. "I can put Chigauroth back to sleep with the spherule, but I have to remain here to do so."

Mu'dai reached for the pendant. "Then let me do it. You only got the orb because I carved it from the witch's hand. It should be me."

Tess held the spherule away, looking back to Mu'dai with sad eyes. "It wouldn't work for you. It needs psychic abilities to function, and you've only a bond with mine."

"Then I'm staying, too!" Mu'dai shouted.

"Oh, how I wish you could, sister," Tess cried. She pointed toward the encroaching wave of flesh along the cavern. "But, until he sleeps again, Chigauroth will consume everything that is Tangleknot, inside and out. Everything but the bearer of the spherule. I am the new Widow of Tangleknot Cave."

"I don't care, I—" Mu'dai began, but Tess kicked her square in the chest, knocking her out of the cave entrance some fifteen feet to the ground below. With no air in her lungs, Mu'dai could do naught but cry, gasping, as she looked up into her sister's own tear-strewn face.

People talked for years afterward about the day the mountain range that housed Tangleknot Cave just appeared, towering over the landscape. Its rocky exterior seemed overrun with tattered flesh, and it almost began to walk. Then, with a twitch here and wrinkle there, the entire mountain began to fold in on itself, eating away until it was gone completely.

*   *   *

Mu'dai felt the loss of Tess immediately. She lay in that unknown field for hours after Tangleknot Cave had disappeared, looking into that foreign sky until the stars came out to prove what she knew to be true. Then, she got up and moved forward. Mu'dai replayed her sister's goodbye message in her memory whenever she felt really low until the end of her days.

This is not forever, Mu'dai. Forever does not start until we are together again, however long that might be. I'll survive with your borrowed strength as you will with mine. I don't know where I'll end up or what you'll go through to find that place, but I know we'll be together again. Scorpion and Crow: the sisters who thwarted a rapist, a witch, and a god, all in one day. With naught but daggers.

www.ingramcontent.com/pod-product-compliance
Lightning Source LLC
Chambersburg PA
CBHW072028170626
46811CB00008B/2987